French Bulldog PUPPIES

by David and Patricia Armentrout

A Crabtree Seedlings Book

TABLE OF CONTENTS

French Bulldog Puppies......................... 3

Glossary 22

Index 24

School-to-Home Support for Caregivers and Teachers

This book helps children grow by letting them practice reading. Here are a few guiding questions to help the reader with building his or her comprehension skills. Possible answers appear here in red.

Before Reading:
- What do I think this book is about?
    - *I think this book is about French bulldog puppies.*
    - *I think this book is about being friends with French bulldog puppies.*
- What do I want to learn about this topic?
    - *I want to learn if I want a French bulldog puppy.*
    - *I want to learn what color French bulldog puppies are.*

During Reading:
- I wonder why…
    - *I wonder why French bulldog puppies have smashed-in faces.*
    - *I wonder why French bulldog puppies' ears stand straight up.*
- What have I learned so far?
    - *I have learned that French bulldog puppies look like their parents.*
    - *I have learned that French bulldog puppies like people.*

After Reading:
- What details did I learn about this topic?
    - *I learned that French bulldog puppies make good pets.*
    - *I learned that French bulldog puppies come in many colors.*
- Read the book again and look for the vocabulary words.
    - *I see the word **France** on page 3, and the word **snouts** on page 8. The other glossary words are found on pages 22 and 23.*

French Bulldog Puppies

French bulldogs come from **France**.

French bulldogs are sometimes called *Frenchies*.

Frenchie moms usually have three puppies in a **litter**.

The puppies look a lot like their parents.

They have flat **snouts**.

Their big ears stand up.

A French bulldog's **coat** is short.

 Common colors are white, black, **brindle**, and fawn.

Like most puppies, French bulldog pups love to play.

A game of fetch or tug-of-war is good exercise.

Frenchies love to be around people.

Their sweet **nature** makes them great pals!

Glossary

brindle (BRIN-duhl): Brindle is a brown color with streaks of other colors.

coat (KOHT): An animal's coat is its fur or wool.

France (FRANSS): France is a country in Europe.

litter (LIT-ur): A litter is a group of puppies or other animals born at the same time to one mother.

nature (NAY-chur): An animal's nature is the usual way it acts.

snouts (SNOUTS): Snouts include the nose, mouth, and jaws on the head of animals.

Index

coat 12
ears 10
litter 4
moms 4
play 14
snouts 8

About the Authors
David and Patricia Armentrout
David and Patricia spend as much time as possible playing and caring for Gimli, Artie, and Scarlet, three special family dogs.

Websites
www.akc.org/dog-breeds/best-dogs-for-kids
www.goodhousekeeping.com/life/pets/g5138/best-family-dogs

Crabtree Publishing

crabtreebooks.com   800-387-7650
Copyright © 2022 Crabtree Publishing

All rights reserved. No part of this publication may be reproduced, stored in a retrieval system or be transmitted in any form or by any means, electronic, mechanical, photocopying, recording, or otherwise, without the prior written permission of Crabtree Publishing Company. In Canada: We acknowledge the financial support of the Government of Canada through the Canada Book Fund for our publishing activities.

Format	ISBN
Hardcover	978-1-4271-5758-4
Paperback	978-1-4271-5759-1
Ebook (pdf)	978-1-4271-5760-7
Epub	978-1-4271-5761-4
Read-along	978-1-4271-5762-1
Audio book	978-1-4271-5763-8

Printed in the U.S.A./112023/PP20230920

Library and Archives Canada Cataloguing in Publication
Title: French bulldog puppies / by David and Patricia Armentrout.
Names: Armentrout, David, 1962- author. | Armentrout, Patricia, 1960- author.
Description: Series statement: Puppy pals | "A Crabtree seedlings book". | Includes index.
Identifiers: Canadiana (print) 20210190922 |
    Canadiana (ebook) 20210190930 |
    ISBN 9781427157584 (hardcover) |
    ISBN 9781427157591 (softcover) |
    ISBN 9781427157607 (HTML) |
    ISBN 9781427157614 (EPUB) |
    ISBN 9781427157621 (read-along ebook)
Subjects: LCSH: French bulldog—Juvenile literature. |
    LCSH: Puppies—Juvenile literature.
Classification: LCC SF429.F8 A76 2022 | DDC j636.72—dc23

Published in Canada
Crabtree Publishing
616 Welland Avenue
St. Catharines, Ontario
L2M 5V6

Published in the United States
Crabtree Publishing
347 Fifth Avenue
Suite 1402-145
New York, NY 10016

Written by: David and Patricia Armentrout
Designed by: Jennifer Dydyk
Edited by: Kelli Hicks
Proofreader: Crystal Sikkens

Photographs: Cover: shutterstock.com/Liliya Kulianionak. background art shutterstock.com/ Dreamzdesigners. Title Page: istock.com/JStaley401. Pages 2-3: istock.com/eliaaa. Pages 4-5: shutterstockc.com/Alice Rodnova. Pages 6: shutterstock.com/Patryk Kosmider Pages 7: shutter stock.com/ Unchalee Khun. Pages 8-9: istock.com/fotokostic. Pages 10: shutterstock.com/ cynoclub. Pages 11: shutterstock.com/dodafoto. Pages 12-13: shutterstock.com/Little Hand Creations. Pages 14-15: istock.com/JStaley401. Pages 16-17: shutterstock.com/TingHelder. Pages 18-19: shutterstock.com/Monkey Business Images. Pages 20-21: istock.com/VVPhoto and DuxX. Page 22 middle photo shutterstock.com/ Sbolotova, map shutterstock.com/seamuss

Library of Congress Cataloging-in-Publication Data
Names: Armentrout, David, 1962- author. | Armentrout, Patricia, 1960- author.
Title: French bulldog puppies / David Armentrout, Patricia Armentrout.
Description: New York : Crabtree Publishing, 2022. |
    Series: Puppy pals - a Crabtree seedlings book | Includes index.
Identifiers: LCCN 2021017151 (print) | LCCN 2021017152 (ebook) |
    ISBN 9781427157584 (hardcover) |
    ISBN 9781427157591 (paperback) |
    ISBN 9781427157607 (ebook) |
    ISBN 9781427157614 (epub) |
    ISBN 9781427157621
Subjects: LCSH: French bulldog--Juvenile literature. | Puppies--Juvenile literature.
Classification: LCC SF429.F8 A76 2022 (print) | LCC SF429.F8 (ebook) |
    DDC 636.72--dc23
LC record available at https://lccn.loc.gov/2021017151
LC ebook record available at https://lccn.loc.gov/2021017152